God Gave Us Angels

God Gave Us Angels

by Lisa Tawn Bergren • art by Laura J. Bryant

SCHOLASTIC INC.

ISBN 978-0-545-91226-6

Text copyright © 2014 by Lisa Tawn Bergren.
Illustrations copyright © 2014 by Laura J. Bryant. All rights reserved.
Scriptures quotations or paraphrases are taken from the Holy Bible, New International Version®, NIV®. Copyright © 1973, 1978, 1984, by Biblica, Inc.™ Used by permission of Zondervan. All rights reserved worldwide. Published by Scholastic Inc., 557 Broadway, New York, NY 10012, by arrangement with WaterBrook Press, an imprint of the Crown Publishing Group, a division of Penguin Random House LLC. SCHOLASTIC and associated logos are trademarks and/or registered trademarks of Scholastic Inc.

12 11 10 9 8 7 6 5 4 3 2 1   15 16 17 18 19 20/0

Printed in the U.S.A.   40

First Scholastic printing, November 2015

Cover design by Mark D. Ford; cover illustration by Laura J. Bryant

For all Little Cubs,
everywhere...

"What are you doing up here, Little Cub?" Papa Bear asked.

"Lookin' for angels," she said in a hushed voice. "The bunnies said they're *all around* us."

"Ahhh," Papa said. "Did you see any?"

"Not yet. But Mama says they're hard
to find. They're *imbisible*."

"Most of the time, they *are* invisible.
But not always."

"Have *you* ever seen one?" Little Cub asked.
"I mean, for reals?"

"I haven't, but I agree with the bunnies.
They're often with us."

"Are some here now?" she whispered.

"Maybe," he whispered back.

"What do angels do all day, Papa?"

"Angels live to serve God. Whatever he wants them to do, they do. And he loves us. So sometimes they bring messages from him to us. Other times they guard us or even fight for us. And they're always worshiping God."

"Does all that worshipin' give them those halo thingies?"

"They don't actually have halos. Artists just show them that way because angels hang out with God so much, they sometimes glow with his light."

"Glow like a lantern?"

Papa laughed. "Kind of. Some have said that seeing an angel is like looking at the sun. They can appear like the biggest, strongest bears you've ever met. Some angels even carry a flaming sword."

"A flaming *sword*?" Little Cub said. "I want one of those!"

"Me too," Papa said with a laugh. "But only angels get to carry them."

"Angels can look so much like us,
we wouldn't even notice them.
That's one reason why we should be
nice to everyone we meet, because
some might be angels in disguise."

"In *disguise*?" she said. "They play dress-up like me?"

"In a way. Sometimes they like to blend in and not distract us. To see if we're willing to take care of others in need—those who might be sick or hungry or without a place to stay."

"Huh. The bunnies said they were our guardians or somethin'."

"There *are* angels that protect us. Sometimes God sends them to keep us from harm. And sometimes he just uses plain ol' parents!"

"But I'm not *always* safe," Little Cub said. "I've gotten hurt. Why didn't God give me an angel those times?"

"I'm not sure, Little Cub. But no matter what happens, we can trust he is near and watching. He loves us, even more than the angels do."

"Should we pray to angels? You know, to ask them to help us?"

"Angels are God's servants. He's their boss. We should pray
only to God, because he is the one who tells them what to do."

"The bunnies say the angels are always singing.
But I can't hear 'em."

"That's because they're up in heaven. I bet they
sing because their hearts are so full," Papa said.
"Can you imagine being able to see God?
Touch him? Know him, like we know each
other? That would make us the happiest bears
alive. We'd be smiling and singing too."

"Will we get to be angels when we die?"

"Nope. Angels have lived with God for a very long time and always will. They were there when he created the earth! We will always be bears. But we'll see angels in heaven for sure."

"God really created angels to serve *him* more than us, Little Cub. They love him and would do anything for him."

Little Cub was quiet. "I love God too."

"I know, Little Cub. So do I."

"I hope I get to see an angel sometime," Little Cub said. "You know. For reals. Then I could tell those bunnies."

Papa smiled. "When you do, you'll catch a glimpse of God's glory and what we'll see in heaven. But until then, I'm going to pray that God sends his angels to watch over you, whether you can see them or not."

Little Cub went to sleep that night and dreamed of singing with the angels and worshiping God. And she was glad, so glad, that God gave them all, angels.